SUPERNATURAL

Mini Guide
to Saving People and
Hunting Things

INSIGHT ◉ EDITIONS

San Rafael, California

THE WINCHESTERS

SAM WINCHESTER

On November 2, 1983, a baby named Sam Winchester was visited by a yellow-eyed demon that dripped its blood into the infant's mouth. Sam's mother, Mary, tried to stop the demon but was killed. This traumatic event se the Winchester family on the path to becoming a clan of unstoppabl monster hunters.

MARY WINCHESTER

Mary Winchester, née Campbell, lived a life of adventure before she met John. Her parents, Samuel and Deanna Campbell, were hunters, as was most of her family before her, stretching back generations. Mary kept her past secret from John for fear of losing him or worse. Unfortunately, her fears were warranted.

ADAM, THE UNKNOWN WINCHESTER

Adam Milligan is the son of Kate Milligan and John Winchester, though he didn't meet his father until he was twelve and only found out about the existence of supernatural monsters when he was killed by a ghoul. Adam later became the archangel Michael's vessel and is now trapped with Lucifer and Michael in Lucifer's cage in Hell.

BAMBOO DAGGER

ills ōkami (fanged Japanese
onsters who feed on humans) if
's properly blessed by a Shinto
riest, but the monster must be
abbed exactly seven times, or it
not truly dead.

BLOOD

Dead humans' blood poisons vampires; dog's blood poisons some pagan gods (such as Veritas the Goddess of Truth); dragon's blood is needed to kill dragons; lamb's blood is needed to kill djinn. Blood is also an essential ingredient in most summoning and banishment spells.

CURSE BOXES

eeps cursed objects from
ffecting those who handle the
oxes. Essential when dealing
ith magical items but must be
cked properly.

DEVIL'S TRAP

A Devil's Trap is a supernatural sigil used to trap demons and bind them in place. It can be drawn with anything from paint to flaming blueberry vodka. However, the instant the sigil's lines are broken in the slightest, the demon can escape. Devil's Traps can also be handy as deterrents to keep demons out of places like car trunks, storage lockers, and panic rooms.

"I've been following you around my entire life. I mean, I've been looking up to you since I was four, Dean. Studying you, trying to be just like my big brother. So yeah, I know you. Better than anyone else in the entire world."

—SAM WINCHESTER

DEAN WINCHESTER

Dean Winchester is the elder Winchester brother. After Mary's death, John Winchester took his sons on the road across the United States on his quest for revenge. Hunting Azazel, the Yellow-Eyed Demon, and killing other evil creatures the family encounters along the way is the perfect life for Dean: He's a good son and a good soldier.

"Once a wise man told me,
'Family don't end in blood.' But it
doesn't start there either. Family
cares about you. Not what you
can do for them. Family is there
for the good, bad, all of it. They
got your back. Even when it hurts.
That's family."

—DEAN WINCHESTER

JOHN WINCHESTER

John Winchester married the love of his life, Mary Campbell, and they had two sons, Dean and Sam. But that's where the fairy tale ended and the nightmare began, with Mary's murder by Azazel in Sam's nursery. Seeking vengeance, John devotes his life to hunting the demon.

HENRY WINCHESTER

Henry was John Winchester's father and therefore Dean and Sam's grandfather. He first met his grandchildren when he was sent to the year 2013 after fleeing the demon Abaddon back in 1958. Henry, like his father before him, was one of the Men of Letters, a group of learned people who study, research, and combat all things supernatural.

"I didn't know my son as a man
but having met you two, I know
would have been proud of him.
—HENRY WINCHESTER

THE WINCHESTER CAR

The Winchesters' car is an automatic, four-door hardtop with a black exterior that does double duty as stylish transportation and sleeping quarters for Sam and Dean. Passed down to Dean by his father, the sleek black car has been lovingly customized by both Winchesters over the years.

The car is perfect for hunting as the trunk can hold a massive weapons arsenal, two duffel bags of clothes, and a body (human or monster). More important, it has a cassette player radio—iPod jacks are not welcome.

"Driver picks the music;
shotgun shuts his cakehole."

—DEAN WINCHESTER

KANSAS
KAZ 2Y5

IRIDIUM

xes, bullets, knives, swords, etc.

ills alpha monsters. As alpha
onsters are rare and hard to kill,
is essential that your iridium-
rged weapon is clean and sharp.

THE WEAPONS
CACHE

There are countless things hidden in the weapons cache found in the car's trunk, but a few items can be found in the car almost all of the time, including Sam and Dean's favorite handguns, a flare gun used to kill a wendigo the brothers encountered, the stake used to "kill" the Trickster, and a knife passed down to Dean from John Winchester.

AFTERMARKET ACCESSORIES

Rosary
Knives
Assorted blades
Wooden stakes
Hex bags
Shotguns
Rifles
Pistols
Axe
Holy water
Dream catcher

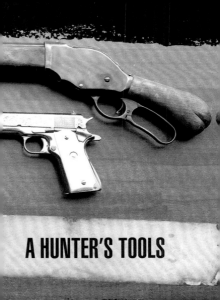

A HUNTER'S TOOLS

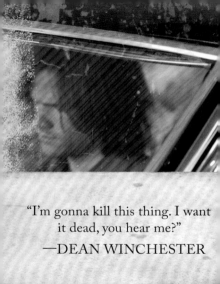

"I'm gonna kill this thing. I want it dead, you hear me?"

—DEAN WINCHESTER

AXE

An essential weapon for a hunter, as it can be used to decapitate monsters (such as vampires and Leviathan—creatures created by God and imprisoned due to their unstable nature).

BRASS

Blades, steam organ pipes, etc.

Kills rakshasa (shapeshifting demons who feed on human flesh); it also has repelling properties.

BRONZE BLADE

Kills sirens, primarily, but it is also a convenient weapon when dealing with "regular" monsters.

CAMERA

A camera's flash will briefly immobilize creatures that are used to the dark; the viewfinder reveals ghosts and the flare in shapeshifters' or other types of monsters' eyes.

CHAIN SAW

Decapitates most monsters and will momentarily incapacitate just about any creature until it can be killed.

CREAM

Inebriates faeries, according to ancient lore and firsthand experience by Dean and Sam Winchester.

CROSSBOW

Depends on the supernatural strength of the monsters, but regular projectile usage applies.

ELECTROMAGNETIC FIELD (EMF) METER

Locates ghosts and is perhaps one of the most essential tools a hunter can have in their arsenal. Most are homemade.

FIRE

Blowtorches, disposable lighters, flare guns, matches, etc.

Kills changelings, crocotta (creatures that take human form to feed on humans' souls), ghouls rugaru (flesh-eating monsters), and wendigos. Fire is a natural tool for hunters, given that most creatures are susceptible to it.

GUN

Handguns, shotguns, sniper rifles, etc.

Slows down just about any monster and, with the proper ammo, can also kill them. Regular bullets can kill Amazons, witches, ghouls, and zombies.

HEX BAG

Hides the bearer from demons.
Can also be used to wreak havoc
if hidden in a person's home,
vehicle, or clothing.

HOLY WATER

Harms and repels demons. Can be used by direct application or by wetting weapons with the blessed liquid.

INSIGHT
EDITIONS

PO Box 3088
San Rafael, CA 94912
www.insighteditions.com

Find us on Facebook:
www.facebook.com/InsightEditions
Follow us on Twitter: @insighteditions

978-1-68383-589-9

Manufactured in China by Insight Editions

10 9 8 7 6 5 4 3 2

"This book. This is Dad's single most valuable possession. Everything he knows about every evil thing is in here. And he's passed it on to us. I think he want us to pick up where he left off. You know, saving people, hunting things. The family business."

—DEAN WINCHESTER

"We're the guys that
save the world."

—SAM WINCHESTER

baby Sam, only to be murdered herself by Azazel years later.

- Christian (cousin): Gets possessed by a demon and spies on his hunting kin, then killed by the Alpha Vampire.
- Gwen (cousin): Killed by Dean, who was infected by the Khan worm.
- Johnny: Killed by a djinn.
- Mark: Killed by the Alpha Shapeshifter.
- Ed and Robert: Killed by Azazel to keep John Winchester off the demon's trail.

the losing side of some battles, leaving Sam and Dean the only members left to honor their family's hunting legacy:

- Deanna (grandmother): Killed by Azazel.
- Samuel (grandfather): Possessed and killed by Azazel. Resurrected by Crowley and makes a deal with the Crossroads Demon, but Sam kills him when he is infected by the Khan worm.
- Mary (mother): Mary makes a deal with Azazel, trading John Winchester's life for access to

hacking the heads off of vampires on the *Mayflower*.

Despite their hunting pedigree, they are not immune to demonic dangers. The Campbell family has found themselves on

The Campbell family, including Mary and her parents, Deanna and Samuel Campbell, were all hunters long before John Winchester became one. The Campbells are a family line of hunters going back further than the first settlers of the United States, some of whom were

THE CAMPBELLS: HUNTERS OF OLD

AMELIA RICHARDSON

Amelia was a veterinarian who worked at the River Bluff Veterinary Hospital. Sam and Amelia struck up a friendship that blossomed into something deeper. They eventually shared a house together for almost a year before Amelia discovered that her husband, who she believed died in Afghanistan, was in fact alive. This revelation led Sam to leave Texas so that Amelia could have a chance to reconnect with her husband.

CHARLIE BRADBURY

One of the Winchester brothers' most unique and talented allies, Charlie continues to aid Sam and Dean when she can with her computer skills. The brothers are always happy to see Charlie, as the cases she is involved in tend to be welcome breaks from the larger struggles that they face. She is like the little sister they never had.

KEVIN TRAN

Kevin is the latest Prophet of the Lord thanks to his contact with the angel tablet, the object previously sought by former Leviathan leader Dick Roman. He can translate the angel and demon tablets. He finds himself working with the Winchester brothers despite his reluctance at being drawn into their never-ending battle with the forces of evil.

elationship with Dean was one of
he closest the elder Winchester
rother had had with a non–
amily member for some time, but
Benny meets his demise helping
Sam escape.

BENNY LAFITTE

Benny was a vampire trapped in Purgatory who became a friend and ally of Dean Winchester during his time there. Despite Dean's mistrust of vampires, Benny quickly proved himself a worthy ally, and the two worked together to both protect each other and formulate a plan to escape.

Once back on Earth, Dean and Benny remained in regular communication and helped each other out when needed. Benny's

...ries to trade the Colt for her soul, ...giving it to Lilith's right-hand man, ...Crowley. But he keeps the Colt ...nstead, and Bela goes to Hell.

BELA TALBOT

Bela Talbot is a master thief with a special knack for communicating with ghosts. She specializes in stealing and selling supernatural objects. When she steals a cursed rabbit's foot from John Winchester's storage unit, she runs afoul of Sam and Dean.

Bela later steals the Colt from the brothers. She had made a deal with a Crossroads Demon when she was younger in exchange for having her abusive parents killed. When her contract comes due, she

GORDON WALKER

Gordon Walker became a hunter obsessed with killing vampires when his sister was turned into a bloodsucker. He thinks all vampires are evil without exception. However, Gordon comes to believe that Sam is the Antichrist and becomes so focused on killing him that even being turned into a vampire himself doesn't distract him from what he believes to be his righteous mission.

Frank's continued research to Leviathan leader Dick oman's activities makes him a rget, and the last Sam and Dean e of him is a mobile trailer full f blood.

FRANK DEVEREAUX

Frank Devereaux is not exactly
a hunter. He's not exactly sane,
either, but he is a very useful ally.
When the Leviathan learn all of
Sam and Dean's aliases, Frank
provides them with new identities
and coaches them on ways to keep
a lower profile; he even teaches
Dean how to hack into security
camera feeds.

to watch out for supernatural-
related cases on behalf of Dean
and Sam.

JODY MILLS

Sheriff Jody Mills didn't start
out wanting to be a hunter. Even
after seeing her undead son eat
her husband and having to shoot
said son in the head, Jody doesn't
actively pursue hunting. She does
however, change her opinion of
Bobby, whom she used to think
was nothing more than a crazy
drunk.

In fact, sparks fly between Jody
and Bobby. Bobby's death comes
as a shock to her, but it motivates
her to use her police connections

GARTH

Another very different hunter acquaintance of Bobby's is Garth Monsters don't get ganked by Garth; they get "Garthed." He usually hunts alone, but he has his sock puppet, Mr. Fizzles, to keep him company. At the end of a hunt, Garth doesn't relax at a place like Harvelle's—he's literally a one-drink drunk—he'd much rather ease his weary bones in a hot tub. When he does hunt with friends, he never lets them part ways without a good hug.

RUFUS TURNER

Due to whatever unspeakable thing happened in the past with Bobby in Omaha, Rufus Turner is somewhat reluctant ally. The two still turn to each other for help with tasks, but their friendship unexpectedly ends when Bobby becomes possessed by a monster and kills Rufus.

Ash's love of the Roadhouse is his downfall, as he dies inside it when it's burned down. But he carries on in Heaven, where his personal version of the afterlife looks like Harvelle's, and his computer now tracks angels instead of demons.

ASH

Harvelle's Roadhouse welcomes
a regular flow of hunters through
its doors, but one customer—
Ash—likes it there so much that
he sleeps in a back room or on the
pool table. Even though he got
kicked out of MIT for fighting,
he's a hacker, not a fighter, so
he does his hunting through
his computer. He even created
specialized demon-tracking
software.

Over time she becomes a truly kickass hunter, even teaming up with her mother on occasion. In the battle against Lucifer, Jo is mortally wounded by Meg's Hellhound and dies in her mother's arms.

JO HARVELLE

Jo Harvelle rebels against her mother, running away from the Roadhouse to follow in her father's hunting footsteps. She's handy with knives and shotguns but inexperienced with actual hunting, and she almost dies on her first case at the hands of a serial killer ghost before the Winchesters save her.

However, it's a matter of "Do as I say, not as I do," because Ellen is a top-notch hunter in her own right and helps Bobby close the Devil's Gate. Years later, she sacrifices her life to help Sam and Dean (try to) kill Lucifer.

ELLEN HARVELLE

Aside from networking through
Bobby, hunters have been known
to exchange horror stories over
brews at Harvelle's Roadhouse.
Ellen Harvelle is the owner and
operator. Her husband, Bill,
died while on a hunt with John
Winchester, and she has tried
to keep her daughter, Jo, from
becoming a hunter.

"Hell, I'm already dead,
what's the worst that could
happen?"

—BOBBY SINGER

With everything he's been through, Bobby no doubt expected to be eaten by a monster someday, but he loses his life to a regular bullet. Yet, even in death Bobby is not willing to lose everything. He hangs on to his life as a ghost haunting his old flask. However, the risk of becoming a vengeful spirit is too great and he insists Sam and Dean burn the flask, and Bobby leaves the Winchesters' lives forever.

Bobby became a hunter after he had to kill his demon-possessed wife, Karen. He was shown the ropes by Rufus Turner whom he hunted with until "the incident" in Omaha. Even when he stays home, he can't avoid hunting, occasionally getting attacked by ghosts and zombies.

BOBBY SINGER

There is one person hunters turn to when they need help or want to network with other hunters: Bobby Singer. Bobby is a surrogate father to Sam and Dean Winchester. When he's not hunting, researching supernatural threats, answering the phone in the guise of a varie of fake federal agents, or buildir monster-proof panic rooms, he runs an auto salvage yard.

ADDITIONAL HUNTERS
AND ALLIES

Leviathan can actually stop other Leviathan. There is a hierarchy to their society, in which underlings are often eaten if they displease their superiors. A particularly cruel punishment, known as bibbing, involves a Leviathan being forced to eat themselves. But there's little chance of the Leviathan eating one another into extinction—not when there are billions of humans ripe for the picking.

In their natural state, they appear as a black goo that can travel through fluids, but once they possess a human body, they are able to shapeshift into any other human they touch. Their large, sharp tooth–filled mouths can expand to engulf a person's head. They have superstrength and regenerate quickly from wounds.

LEVIATHAN

Long before God created angels and humans, he made the first beasts: the Leviathan. Clever and nearly invulnerable, they had a bad habit of eating everything God subsequently created. They even killed angels, leading God to create a Purgatory in which to lock the Leviathan away—until Castiel inadvertently let them back into the world.

Lucifer gathers them to him in preparation of the Apocalypse. War, Famine, and Pestilence don't seem to mind following Lucifer's orders, but Death—who is far more powerful than the other Horsemen—does not like being bound to Lucifer. He willingly gives Dean his ring, as the combined rings are the key to sending Lucifer back to his cage in Hell.

All of the Horsemen can teleport, and they each have special supernatural talents:

War reads minds and gives people hallucinations that make them fight with one another.

Famine consumes souls (human or demon) and makes people so hungry for the things they crave the most that they're willing to kill for them.

Pestilence creates horrific and incurable diseases; and Death commands reapers and raises the dead.

horse and a sickly green AMC
Hornet; and Death a white horse
and a white Cadillac Eldorado.

THE
FOUR HORSEMEN

The Four Horsemen—War, Famine, Pestilence, and Death—are destructive forces of nature. When they show themselves to humans, they do so with great dramatic flare. War has been seen riding a red horse and driving a red Ford Mustang; Famine a black horse and a black Cadillac Escalade; Pestilence a pale green

"Why not just serve your own best interests? Which in this case just happen to be mine?"

—LUCIFER

veals his greatest weakness:
nity. He overestimates his
ppression of Sam's will and
nderestimates the power of
milial love, losing control of
am's body just long enough for
am to drag him back to Hell.

He did, however, create demons, and for that God imprisoned him in Hell. Lucifer truly believes that he was wronged by God for not bowing down to humans, who he sees as flawed, violent, fragile little creatures. When Sam Wincheste frees him from his cage, Lucifer wants revenge on humans, on his archangel brothers, and on God himself.

After he convinces Sam to become his new vessel, Lucifer

LUCIFER:
KING OF HELL

Lucifer. Satan. The Devil. Beelzebub. Serpent King. Lord of the Flies. Prince of Darkness. Father of Lies. Ruler of Hell. Call him what you will—just don't call him a demon, as he is actually a fallen archangel.

he final seal: Lilith dies. As it is
ritten, "The first demon will be
e last seal."

THE 66 SEALS

What are they? Locks on the door of Lucifer's Cage.

How many are there? 600

How do they work? Break 66 an Lucifer is freed from Hell.

Is there a combination? The first and last are crucial, but the middle 64 can be any of the other 598.

The first seal: The first seal is broken when a righteous man—i this case Dean Winchester— sheds blood in Hell.

ZACHARIAH

As part of Heaven's upper management, Zachariah was consistently employee of the month in Heaven before his failure to recruit Sam and Dean Winchester as vessels for Lucifer and Michael made him a laughingstock. Zachariah thinks his luck's finally changed when Dean agrees to become Michael's vessel, only to discover it was a ruse for Dean to get close enough to kill him with an angel blade.

VIRGIL

Virgil is an angel assassin that Raphael sends to retrieve the heavenly weapons from Balthaza but the crafty rogue angel whips up a spell that sends Virgil chasing after the Winchester brothers to an alternate universe, where he remains trapped to this day.

URIEL

An angel purification specialist who feels that dealing with humans is a waste of his time. He claims he can turn humans to dust just by uttering one word, but he is kept in line by Castiel. Uriel secretly plots to break seals and kills any angels that refuse to help him free Lucifer. Once he fails to convert Castiel to his cause, he plans to make him his next victim, but Anna kills Uriel first.

When Castiel takes on God-like powers of his own thanks to the souls from Purgatory, Raphael is simply wiped out of existence by a snap of the now-powerful angel's fingers.

RAPHAEL

Raphael is a staunch supporter of his archangel brother Michael. After the first seal is broken, he does everything he can to bring on the Apocalypse so that Michael and Lucifer can end their eons-old spat once and for all. He won't let anything stop him—not even Castiel, whom he kills and then continues to war with in his resurrected form.

NAOMI

A powerful agent from Heaven's intelligence division, Naomi was ruthless in her quest to prevent the angel tablet from falling into the wrong hands. She was the one who brought Castiel back from Purgatory and used him as her spy on Earth until he rebelled and severed his connection to her. She was killed by Metatron.

MICHAEL

As the oldest and most powerful archangel, Michael wants Lucifer to rise from Hell so that they can have an apocalyptic grudge match. But Castiel interrupts his plans when he destroys Michael's planned human vessel (Adam Milligan) with Holy Fire, and the Sam Winchester yanks Michael down into Lucifer's cage in Hell, where the two angels wrestle on in a never-ending battle.

METATRON

Metatron was an angel scribe wh[o]
recorded the Word of God on tw[o]
tablets that have since become
weapons in the war between
angels and the demons. When th[e]
archangels realized they needed
both Metatron and the two
tablets to take over the universe
themselves, Metatron fled to
Earth, where he sequestered
himself in a Colorado motel and
plotted his revenge.

JOSHUA

Joshua is Heaven's gardener.
Even as most angels are starting
to feel like God has left the
building, Joshua claims to have
conversations with God, though
they're mostly one-way. When th
brothers are trapped in Heaven,
he saves Sam and Dean from
Zachariah in order to deliver
a message to them from God
Himself.

HESTER

member of Castiel's former
ngel garrison in Heaven.
elieving Castiel to be dead,
e arrives on Earth to protect
e new Prophet of the Lord,
evin Tran, from harm. Hester
shocked to learn that Castiel is
ive, but she is eventually killed
Meg when she tries to kill
astiel.

e was just a disposable pawn
Metatron's plan to become
he new God. He finally found
edemption by sacrificing himself
o that Castiel could put a stop to
Metatron's master plan.

GADREEL

The angel Gadreel was one of
God's most trusted angels and wa
tasked with protecting Paradise.
When he failed in this task, he
was imprisoned in one of Heaven'
darkest dungeons for thousands
of years. When Metatron's spell
expelled all the angels from
Heaven, Gadreel was freed.

Gadreel pretended to be the
much-respected angel Ezekiel an
promised to help the Winchester
brothers, but he ultimately joined
Metatron's cause before realizing

GABRIEL

Gabriel is the archangel formerly known as the Trickster. He disguised himself as the pagan god Loki in order to hide from his squabbling brothers, Michael and Lucifer, but he nonetheless takes a special interest in the human brothers destined to become Michael and Lucifer's vessels, Dean and Sam Winchester.

His relationship with the Winchesters eventually causes him to take the side of the humans and battle Lucifer, dying valiantly.

"Now I realize that there is no righteous path, it's just people trying to do their best in a worl where it is far too easy to do your worst."

—CASTIEL

nds in his way. Later, he

sorbs the evil creatures known

Leviathan; unable to contain

em, he implodes, freeing them

roam the planet.

Castiel returns, months later,

changed angel who cannot

member his past. Eventually,

hile working with the

Vinchesters, he remembers who

is and embarks on a quest to

ght his wrongs.

He can also travel to the past
become invisible to humans,
incinerate monsters, and smite
demons with a simple touch. In
the Winchesters' fight against ev
Castiel is an invaluable ally. But
he is not without his flaws. His
bond with Dean and his affectio
for humans makes him weak in
the eyes of other angels.

Castiel touchingly proves
himself a little bit human along
the way, until he declares himsel
the new God and destroys
anyone—and anything—that

CASTIEL

Angel. Soldier of God. Defender of humans. Castiel is all these things and more, and from his very first appearance, he has established himself as one of the most powerful and intriguing figures to enter the Winchesters' lives. His powers are vast, proven from the beginning, when he pulled Dean out of the very depths of Hell to once again walk the Earth and fulfill his mission to stop the impending Apocalypse.

BARTHOLOMEW

he angel Bartholomew was
rhaps the biggest thorn in
astiel's side. After falling to
arth, Bartholomew consolidated
s power by finding human
ssels to contain thousands of
splaced angels, thus creating an
nstoppable army.

Castiel refused to ally with
artholomew and was able to
erpower and kill him. Realizing
astiel represented the best way
rward, many of Bartholomew's
llowers declared their allegiance
the rebel angel.

BALTHAZAR

althazar once fought alongside
astiel, but he now believes it's
new era with no rules and no
estiny—just utter and complete
eedom. He fakes his own death
live on Earth and remains an
ly of sorts, assisting Castiel a few
mes.

When he discovers Castiel is
orking with the demon Crowley,
e spies on his friend for the
Vinchesters and pays for his
etrayal when he's literally stabbed
the back by Castiel.

She goes on the run but eventually returns to save Castiel from the rogue angel Uriel. Castiel, ever the good soldier, still sends Anna to prison in Heaven, but she eventually escapes and travels back in time to try to kill John and Mary Winchester before they can give birth to Sam, Lucifer's vessel. Ironically, Anna gets a younger Uriel to help her, but then the Archangel Michael possesses John and smites her.

ANNA

Anna was Castiel's superior in Heaven, but she ripped out her Grace and fell to Earth so that she could experience love and chocolate. When the first seal on Lucifer's cage is broken, the now-human Anna starts hearing angels broadcasting messages. She wants to remain human, but with demons trying to use her to spy on the angels and angels trying to kill her for removing her Grace she has no choice but to reinsert it

ANGELS FROM
A TO Z

Enochian sigils are glyphs
of immense power used to bind
demons, protect individuals
from angelic detection, and
prevent angels from entering or
discovering spaces such as houses,
rooms, or great swaths of land.

ENOCHIAN

Enochian is the language of angels, which they use to communicate with one another in Heaven and on Earth. It is also used in spells that involve angels whether one is summoning, binding, or expelling them. There is an Enochian chant that can forcibly expel an angel from its human vessel and send it back to Heaven.

ree things that can kill them: a
eviathan, one of their own angel
ades, and the archangels.

There are only four
rchangels—Michael, Lucifer,
aphael, and Gabriel—and they
re God's most terrifying warriors,
le to obliterate a "regular"
ngel with a simple snap of their
ngers.

Angels can teleport at will, knock a human out cold with a touch, and enter a person's dreams. They can even travel through time, but the act takes a enormous physical toll on them.

Although awe-inspiring, they do have some weaknesses: A circle of Holy Fire will trap them and both Holy Fire and heavenly weapons can destroy their human vessels. Plus, there are

en if that means killing other
gels, eradicating thousands
humans, or actually helping
llen archangel Lucifer start the
pocalypse.

Angels are warriors of God. The
are colossal, winged beings that
are multidimensional wavelength
of celestial intent. Their true
forms will burn human eyes out,
and their true voices will shatter
glass and burst human eardrums
so they communicate via
electronics (like TVs and radios)
when necessary. However, they
will usually take on a human hos

Angels can see demons' true
faces and are only too happy to
smite them immediately. Devoid
of free will and human emotions
they'll follow their orders blindly

A GUIDE TO ANGELS

ABBADON

baddon is a demon Knight of
ell and the last of her kind. She
turned to Earth to claim control
Hell from Crowley and turn
l of humankind into her demon
my. She was killed by Dean
hen he used the First Blade on
r.

Lucifer agreed, but only on the condition that Cain kill Abel himself. Cain murdered his brother with a donkey's jawbone, which then became known as the First Blade. Lucifer marked Cain with a special brand that gave the First Blade its power and made Cain a demon—the first of Lucifer's Knights of Hell. Cain then led his fellow Knights as they wreaked havoc across the earth.

CAIN

Centuries ago, Lucifer tried to corrupt Cain's younger brother, Abel, and make the young man his special "pet." In order to prevent this, Cain made a deal with Lucifer that Abel's soul would be kept safe in Heaven in exchange for his own soul, which Lucifer would keep in Hell.

THE KNIGHTS OF HELL

MEG

Meg is Azazel's "daughter" and enters the Winchesters' lives as a potential love interest for Sam, but it isn't long before she reveals that she's a demon. The brothers manage to exorcise her multiple times, but she keeps returning in different bodies.

When Crowley becomes King of Hell, Meg attempts to use Castiel as a weapon against Crowley, but her plan backfires, and she is captured and taken back to Hell.

Ultimately, Ruby helps Sam to
ll Lilith, which appears to be a
od thing until the Winchesters
nd out that Ruby has kept an
mportant fact from them: Killing
ilith breaks the final seal that
ees Lucifer from Hell. Ruby's
ctorious gloating is short-lived,
Sam grabs hold of her and
ean stabs her with her own
emon-killing knife.

RUBY

Ruby is Lilith's most loyal
follower. She initially appears
to be just another hunter—one
who happens to have a knife tha
kills demons. But even when the
Winchesters learn she's a demon
she makes them wonder whethe
she could actually be a good one

- Acheri are demons that disguise themselves as little girls, albeit with superlong fingernails coated in blood.
- The Seven Deadly Sins thrive on causing the sin they represent.
- Samhain, the Lord of the Dead, raises ghosts, ghouls, zombies, and other beasts on All Hallows' Eve.
- Croatoan are virus-sized demons that fill people with demonic rage and are passed by blood-to-blood contact.

Most black-eyed demons are interchangeable, but some demo
stand out:

BLACK-EYED DEMONS

These are the soldiers, thugs, henchmen, and minions—the masses. Most are just mindless drones that do the bidding of Azazel, Lilith, or Crowley without question. But some have very distinct personalities of their own.

By dripping his own demon blood into baby Sam's mouth on the night of Mary's death, Azazel guaranteed the brothers' lives would never be their own. Azazel's endgame was to raise Lucifer from Hell with Sam as his vessel, but he didn't live to accomplish that, thanks to Dean and a silver bullet from the Colt.

AZAZEL

Azazel is the only known Yellow
Eyed Demon and is the catalyst
for everything that Sam and Dean
Winchester have gone through.
He killed their grandparents and
their father, John, whom he then
resurrected in return for future
access to baby Sam. When he killed
Mary Winchester, Sam and Dean
are pushed farther into becoming
hunters.

YELLOW-EYED DEMONS

These are the demon army generals.

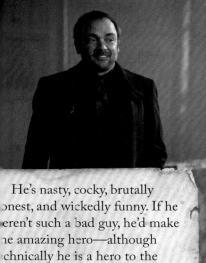

He's nasty, cocky, brutally
onest, and wickedly funny. If he
eren't such a bad guy, he'd make
e amazing hero—although
chnically he is a hero to the
rces of evil.

CROWLEY

Crowley is Lilith's right-hand man and King of the Crossroads As a human he was a Scottish tailor named Fergus Roderick McLeod who sold his soul for three additional inches below the waist. His wish-granting capabilities seem to have no limits. After Lilith and Alastair are killed and Lucifer is locked up again, Crowley crowns himse the King of Hell.

RED-EYED DEMONS

hese are the Crossroad Demons,
emon dealmakers who make
eals for the souls that fuel Hell.
hey can grant humans practically
ny wish, making their powers on
ar with reality-altering angels
ke Zachariah. It's unknown
ow many Crossroad Demons
here are, but Crowley is the most
owerful.

ALASTAIR

Alastair is very old and powerful, possibly the second demon ever created. He is Hell's master torturer, and he tortured both John and Dean Winchester when they were in Hell. When Castiel and Alastair battle each other, Alastair gets the upper hand on Castiel and nearly sends him back to Heaven with an Enochian spell, but Sam arrives and uses his psychic demon powers to first torture and then kill Alastair.

Lilith loves Lucifer and willingly
sacrifices herself, allowing Sam to
kill her, knowing that as the first
demon, she is the last seal binding
Lucifer to his cage.

LILITH

Lilith was the first demon ever created. In keeping with her white eyes, her signature attack is a devastating blast of white energy. Because she is the Queen of the Crossroads, all Crossroads Demons make deals for her, which is why she ultimately holds sway over Dean Winchester's soul and plots to use Dean to break the first seal binding Lucifer to his cage.

WHITE-EYED
DEMONS

These demons are the chiefs of staff.

When hunting demons, the
st way to spot them is to look
traces of sulfur, lightning
rms, and cattle mutilations,
ich they tend to leave behind
erever they've been. They can't
ss lines of salt, iron and holy
ter burns them, Palo Santo
oly Wood) can pin them
wn, and a Devil's Trap works as
vertised. Additionally, saying any
God's names will make them
ch and flash their demon eyes.

Exorcisms expel demons from people's bodies, which is useful because it keeps the body intact but doing so just sends the demon back to Hell. It's best to destroy them with a demon-killing knife or shoot them with the Colt, though that will kill their meatsuit as well.

ve superhuman strength and
ekinetic abilities, and they love
torture people.

Demons are human souls that were sent to Hell and became twisted into evil spirits. God preferred humans to angels and Lucifer became jealous. To provoke God, he tempted a human soul and twisted it into the very first demon. This action is what got him locked up in his supernatural cage downstairs.

Demons mostly reside in He but when demons can escape to our world, they rarely stay incorporeal, preferring instead to possess humans, which they refer to as meat-suits. They

THE HIERARCHY OF
DEMONS

"We know a little about a lot of things; just enough to make us dangerous."

—DEAN WINCHESTER

ZOMBIES

 dead person reanimated by
Death or through necromancy.
hey often try to go back to
heir old lives but are driven by
 hunger for revenge and will
appily kill anyone who wronged
hem in life. They seem normal at
rst, but eventually their hunger
or human flesh will escalate,
urning them into a stereotypical
ombie. They can be killed by
aking, beheading, or otherwise
estroying their heads.

Wraiths will die if they go too
ng without feeding on human
sh and can also be killed with a
eapon made of pure silver.

WRAITHS

humanoid creature that gets
ose to other humans in order
eat their brains. A wraith has
spike that pops out of its wrist
hen it's feeding. Wraiths enjoy
e taste of "insane" brains and
e usually found near mental
stitutions. They are capable
causing hallucinations and
her emotional changes through
hysical touch.

WITCHES

Witches are humans who use
dark magic to perform curses,
summon demons, and even
swap bodies. They need to use
various combinations of spells,
sigils, effigies, hex bags, and
animal sacrifices to affect others
magically. Usually, they use magic
to enrich their own lives and
torture their enemies. Witches
can be killed using conventional
weapons.

Whatever you do, don't get
tten. Don't listen to hunters
ho tell you that killing the
erewolf that bit you will lift
e curse, as there is no cure.
Werewolves can only be killed by
silver bullet.

WEREWOLVES

A person infected by lycanthropy will turn into a ravenous, supernaturally strong human-wolf hybrid known as a werewolf during the full moon. Although they act like feral animals, werewolves tend to hunt and kill people who have angered them in their human lives. If it wasn't for this connection, they might never find out they're werewolves as they don't seem to retain any memories of their monstrous behavior.

WENDIGO

 wendigo is an individual
ho has eaten human flesh in
onjunction with black magic
d gained inhuman speed and
rength, as well as immortality.
hey're bigger than humans, their
eth and nails are monstrously
ng, and their eyes glow. To
tch their prey, they lure hikers
ep into the forest and then
old them prisoner in their
nderground lairs until feeding
me. They can only be killed with
re.

They sire new vampires by force-feeding people their infected blood. Crosses do not repel them, and direct sunlight will burn them but not kill them—and nor will a stake through the heart. Vampires can only be killed through beheading.

VAMPIRES

ampires are "turned" humans
ho have extra-sharp, retractable
eth and crave human blood.
hey nest in packs and sleep in
ocoon-style hammocks; they
eed to feed on mammalian blood
 survive, and human blood
stes the best.

SIRENS

Sirens have pale skin, hollow eyes, and a scary mouth, but they usually take on human forms. They can read minds and use what they learn to take on the guise of someone their intended victims will desire being with, then they use their toxic saliva to turn their victims into adoring slaves. The only way to kill a siren is with a bronze dagger dipped in the blood of someone it has infected.

SHTRIGAS

ghastly-looking soul-sucker; htrigas are a type of witch that eds by sucking the "breath of fe" out of people. They prefer ildren because their life forces e strongest, but any human will . They target sick, suicidal, or herwise weak people because eir life forces are not attached strongly to their bodies. They n only be killed by consecrated rought iron.

SHAPESHIFTERS AND SKINWALKERS

These monsters have the ability to transform into exact replicas of humans or animals. They study your routines and mannerisms, then take on your appearance and steal your memories to mimic you perfectly. Some can change their appearance, while others must shed their old skins when their new form emerges. All shapeshifters and skinwalkers can be killed with a silver bullet or other sharp silver object to the heart.

REAPERS

Reapers are spirit-like creatures that usually appear in human form. They reap souls for Death can stop time and alter human perception, and will use any methods they can think of to ge the newly dead to cross over to the afterlife. The living can't see them, so you have to use astral projection, kill yourself to find them, or use an angel or demon your go-between, as they can se reapers easily.

PAGAN GODS

gan gods are supernatural
tities that gain their power
om humans worshipping
em as gods. They like to eat
mans, but they're not greedy;
ey provide their worshippers
th bountiful harvests, good
alth, and protection from other
ngry pagan gods in return for a
atively small number of human
crifices.

KHAN WORM

creation of Eve, the Mother of
l Monsters, the Khan worm is
parasitic worm that crawls into
mans' ears and takes control of
eir bodies. It turns friends and
mily against each other with
adly consequences, and was a
ol developed by Eve as a means
exterminating humankind. It
n be killed with electric current.

GHOULS

Ghouls are monster scavengers that eat the dead and take on the likenesses, thoughts, and memories of their victims' last meal. Usually they dig up graves and eat the corpses, but they may also come after the living. They can only be killed by decapitation or the destruction of their heads.

They're usually tethered to their bones, so if they've been cremated, look for other remains of theirs that would have some DNA attached, like a friendship bracelet with blood on it or a wig made out of their hair or even a donated kidney.

GHOSTS

pirits of the deceased that are
rapped on Earth. They can walk
hrough walls, the stronger ones
an move objects and kill people,
nd they'll haunt just about
nything—loved ones, houses,
otels, mental asylums, cars, boats,
oads, flasks—and some ghosts
an even infect people like a
isease, making them so afraid of
verything that their hearts burst.

he victim's bodily fluids. Djinn
an be killed with a silver knife
ipped in lamb's blood.

DJINN (GENIES)

Essentially evil genies, djinn
are creatures of smokeless fire,
but their solid human form is
indistinguishable from regular
humans. With just a touch, they
make their victim's greatest wish
come true—but only inside their
victims' minds. These supernatur
hallucinations feel so real that
the victims rarely try to wake up
Meanwhile, the djinn will feed o

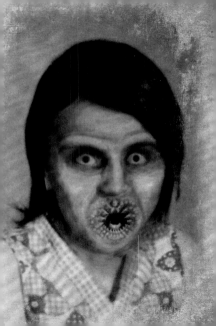

CHANGELINGS

A supernatural creature that mimics the appearance and behavior of human children in order to feed off of their human mothers, and will kill anyone who tries to stop them. The changeling mother will feed the human children who have been abducted and replaced. Changelings can be destroyed by fire, and when the changeling mother is killed, her brood dies with her.

ANTICHRIST

orn of a demon-possessed
rgin human, the Antichrist
possessed of almost limitless
pernatural abilities and can
stroy the "Host of Heaven" with
ingle word. The Antichrist's
wers include telekinesis,
eportation, exorcising demons
th his mind, and making even
e simplest of thoughts a reality.
e Antichrist is impossible to
l but can be persuaded to never
e his powers again if reasoned
th compassionately.

There are too many monsters lurking around every corner to count, much less describe in detail, but what follows is a primer on some of the supernatural beings Dean and Sam have encountered in past years.

THINGS THAT GO BUMP
IN THE NIGHT

kitchen, multiple bedrooms, dungeon, and one hell of a rage, complete with vintage tomobiles from the 1950s.

In addition to a main meetin
room with a large table covered
by an illuminated world map, th
bunker contains a fully stocked
research library, an observatory,
crow's nest, a laboratory,

Upon Henry Winchester's death Sam and Dean became Legacies and inherited the Men of Letter sprawling underground bunker. The bunker is home to the Men of Letters' enormous library of research material, classified files, and enough weaponry and other items for combatting the supernatural to keep Sam and Dean stocked for the rest of thei (un)natural lives.

MEN OF LETTERS BUNKER

Holy Fire can also be used to burn angels out of their vessels or least cause them to teleport to e nearest body of water.

HOLY FIRE

Holy Fire is a very effective weapon for fighting angels as it is Holy Oil set on fire. However, Holy Oil is a rare substance, and its composition and origins are unknown. A circle of Holy Fire will entrap an angel as surely as a Devil's Trap will hold a demon.

ARK OF THE COVENANT

robably the most famous and
ost powerful of all heavenly
eapons. Its true usage is unclear,
ut the Winchester's ally, the
ngel Castiel, doesn't refute that
's in the form of a gold box and
hat looking inside it will melt the
ces off humans. It's the heavenly
quivalent of a supernatural
uclear device.

GABRIEL'S HORN OF TRUTH

When blown, it compels all who hear it to speak the truth.

LOT'S SALT ROCK

Was used on humans when Lot's wife disobeyed the angels' order not to look back at Sodom, the doomed city her family was fleeing. Her eyes fell on the supercharged salt crystal, and she was instantly transformed into a pillar of salt.

…ainst angels in human vessels.
…reviously used by Moses in his
…splay of dominance against the
…gyptians, it is now in less potent
…eces scattered throughout
…eaven.

STAFF OF MOSES

The staff can control water, cover people in boils, and summon a plague of locusts, among other things. The staff can also transform into a snake and is effective

HEAVENLY BLADE

rare modification of the angel
ade, which has been fine-tuned
kill powerful gods like the
ates.

ARCHANGEL BLADE

Looks the same as an angel blade to mortal eyes, but it's been supercharged (presumably from being wielded by an archangel) and is capable of killing even the most powerful of angels.

However, the blade is equally
ficient at killing Hellhounds—
d, no doubt, humans, too.
eavenly power is imbued in
e blade, allowing it to be used
fectively by anyone, including
mons and humans.

ANGEL BLADE

Aka the angel-killing dagger. It's unknown what alloy this weapon is made of, and it's unlikely that its original purpose was to kill angels, but during the war in Heaven, that becomes its primary use.

HEAVENLY WEAPONS

THE FIRST BLADE

Cain, the leader of the Knights of Hell, forged the First Blade from the donkey's jawbone he used to kill his brother, Abel. It is the only known weapon that can kill Abaddon. Cain's mark is the source of the First Blade's power, and he can only transfer it to someone worthy to bear it. Despite the dangers, Dean agrees to wear the mark so that he can wield the blade.

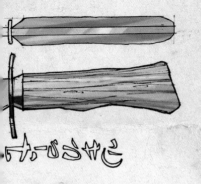

erself since she had the know-
ow to make the Colt work again
ithout Samuel's magic bullets, a
kill she shared with Bobby Singer.

The demon-killing knife's origins
are unknown, and the engravings
on its blade are unknowable,
but it seems likely Ruby made it

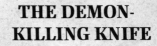

THE DEMON-KILLING KNIFE

Ruby appeared with her special knife that could kill demons—and only demons—as readily as the Colt.

ossession of the weapon, and,
ith John and his sons making full
e of it, the bullets soon ran out.

Legend says this gun can kill anything, although that's not quite true. It kills demons, vampires, and phoenixes without a problem, but it can't kill Lucifer. The fallen archangel claims there are four other things in all of creation it can't kill—likely the other three archangels, and Death.

Samuel Colt made thirteen numbered silver bullets for the gun, of which five remained when John Winchester came into

THE COLT

In 1835, Samuel Colt assembled a very special gun. While its barrel is the key that unlocks the Devil's Gate he built in Wyoming, he ultimately built the weapon for hunting supernatural creatures. It has a pentagram on the handle and is engraved with Latin words that translate to *I will fear no evil.*

SPECIAL WEAPONS

WOODEN STAKE

Made out of Babylonian cypress, evergreen, etc. Kills pagan gods, the Whore of Babylon, and tricksters.

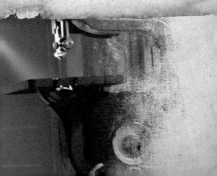

SWORD

Perfect for decapitating monsters (such as Leviathan); kills dragons (when coated in dragons' blood); and kills shōjō (when consecrated by a Shinto blessing).

TASER

Electrocutes rawheads but is also handy for incapacitating a variety of monsters or even belligerent humans.

SUGAR

When sugar is spilled in front of
eries, they have to stop what
hey're doing and count every
rain.

SILVER

Axes, bullets, knives, stakes, swords, etc.

Kills djinn, shapeshifters, skinwalkers, vetalas (creatures that sedate their victims with a toxin and feed on them for days) wendigos, werewolves, wraiths, and zombies. Having silver on hand when facing most monsters and creatures is essential.

RAM'S HORN

Kills some pagan gods (such as Osiris) and can often be found in synagogues.

SALT

Circles of salt and salt lines across entryways can keep out ghosts and demons. Shotgun blasts of rock salt dispel ghosts.

PALO SANTO

Holy wood that is toxic to demons and serves the same purpose as holy water in repelling or harming—but not killing—these creatures of Satan.

MIRROR

Shows the true faces of changelings, sirens, and wraiths, and is a useful tool to quickly reveal the true nature of anybody you suspect to be a monster in disguise.

MACHETE

Ideal for decapitating monsters such as arachne, as well as vampires and Leviathan.

LOCKPICKS

Their use is self-explanatory, but
they are essential tools of the trade
for hunters, so it is important to
keep quite a few in various shapes
and sizes handy.

KNIFE

epends on the supernatural
rength of the monster, but
gular blade usage applies.
standard weapon for every
nter's arsenal.

IRON

xes, buckshot, bullets, chains,
nives, nails, etc.

ispels ghosts; keeps demons,
eries, and phoenixes (creatures
ho turn their victims to ash)
bay or traps them; and kills
trigas and some pagan gods
uch as leshii).